Benny Dubious Playbook Scheme Trouble in Georgia Book 3: Hugo's Revelation

Benny Dubious Playbook Scheme Series 3, Volume 3

Maxwell Hoffman

Published by Maxwell Hoffman, 2024.

BENNY DUBIOUS PLAYBOOK SCHEME TROUBLE IN GEORGIA BOOK 3: HUGO'S REVELATION

First edition. October 19, 2024.

Copyright © 2024 Maxwell Hoffman.

ISBN: 979-8227113122

Written by Maxwell Hoffman.

Also by Maxwell Hoffman

Benny Dubious Playbook Scheme Series 3
Benny Dubious Playbook Scheme Trouble in Georgia: The Moshie
Affair
Benny Dubious Playbook Scheme Trouble in Georgia Book 2:
"Moshie's" Fall
Benny Dubious Playbook Scheme Trouble in Georgia Book 3: Hugo's
Revelation

Ivan Zhuk: Zhuk's Gambit
Ivan Zhuk: Zhuk's Gambit Book 1 Mental Agony

Misadventures of Wolfgang Wirrarr
Misadventures of Wolfgang Wirrarr Omnibus Trilogy

Rowan Sunfire Frosty Fugitive Series
Rowan Sunfire Frosty Fugitive Book 3 Defense of Vos Tower
Rowan Sunfire Frosty Fugitive Omnibus Trilogy

Table of Contents

BENNY DUBIOUS PLAYBOOK SCHEME
TROUBLE IN GEORGIA BOOK 3
HUGO'S REVELATION
by
Maxwell Hoffman

Part One

Prologue

<u>Loud Hebrew Music</u>

#

Benny Dubious was doing his best trying to get through the crowds of people trying to get up to the stage. He was determine to get Hugo Roth out of there while they still could. Agent GA who was in the back stage of the concert was a bit disappointed that Hugo didn't take the opportunity to reveal the truth.

#

"Kid, you're just delaying the inevitable here" sighed Agent GA.

#

The agent gazed upon the crowd and noticed Benny Dubious moving about. What was that Malian crime boss doing? Then the agent figured it out, was he sent here by Samuel Roth to retrieve Hugo? The agent had to find a way to protect Hugo.

#

"Kid just do your best and try to say it when you're ready on stage" added Agent GA, "no pressure."

#

The agent wanted to assure Hugo even while dawning the "Moshie Scheinman" persona one last time that everything was going to be okay. However, there was the matter of handling Benny, for Benny the loud music in Hebrew through the AI computer system made it difficult for him to move about. Crowds of people were blocking his path, but eventually Benny had to use his own muscle to get through.

\#

<u>Pushing People Out of the Way</u>

\#

Benny was determine to get through the row of people, pushing various people aside. It didn't matter if it was a man who was in the way or a woman.

\#

"Hey, watch where you're going you big brute!" bellowed a woman.

\#

"Yea, we were enjoying the concert!" added a man.

\#

The couple picked themselves up and began to try to tackle Benny, Benny was too tough for either of them. He ended up knocking them both out with one blow.

\#

"Didn't want to come to this" sighed Benny.

\#

Benny soon did the same to anyone else who was standing in his path. Agent GA knew he had to act quickly, he soon alerted the Blue Eagle spies in the area to come towards where the commotion was happening within the crowd.

#

"That loser just knocked my friend unconscious!" cried another woman to a male Blue Eagle spy.

#

"We'll handle it" said the male Blue Eagle spy.

#

The Blue Eagle spies began to zero in on Benny, Benny couldn't believe the Blue Eagle Collective were going to finally get him.

#

"Alright, that's enough pushing people around" said a woman Blue Eagle spy, "you can sit back and watch the concert or we'll have to put you under arrest."

#

"There is no way you'll stop me from reaching the main concert" said Benny.

#

Benny soon ducked as a few Blue Eagle spies lunged towards him, he then used their jackets against them by taking them off.

#

<u>Using Jackets as Whips</u>

#

Benny was quite resourceful in this method, using their own clothing as weapons.

#

"Stay back, I'm not afraid to use these" said Benny.

#

Benny eventually managed to push his way towards the crowd, he nearly was reaching towards the front of the concert. He could hear the voice of Ms. Nia Hope Carver and her father - Senator Amos Carver III and her campaign manager - Ms. Ashura Clark.

#

"Yea, that's my boyfriend up on the stage!" laughed Nia.

#

Nia was busy taking selfies with her cellphone. She was posting it all on social media for everyone to see. This was much of the disapproval of her campaign manager.

#

"Uh, so childish" sighed Ashura.

#

Ashura couldn't believe the next generation of leaders would be doing this or possibly worse things to get attention. But much to Ashura's discontent, she took a glance over an app on her cellphone that showed the poll numbers - Nia was catching up!

\#

"This, this is working?!" cried Ashura much to her shock.

\#

Even her father - Senator Amos Carver III was impressed as he took a glance at the poll numbers.

\#

"Yes, this concert is helping her!" laughed Senator Amos, "Can't believe I'm saying this but go Moshie!"

\#

This with despite knowledge over "Moshie Scheinman's" true identity being Hugo Roth, the Senator didn't seem to care at this point. He was just living the moment.

\#

Agent GA Stands in the Way

\#

Meanwhile, for Benny he managed to make it through rows and rows of people. Even having run ins with Blue Eagle Collective spies. However, Benny soon would meet the head of the operations - Agent GA.

\#

"Not so fast Benny Dubious" said Agent GA as he stood before him.

\#

"You don't understand, Samuel's wife Josephine is making me do this" said Benny.

\#

"We know that Samuel's wife doesn't like her husband being involved in politics" said Agent GA.

\#

Agent GA pulled out what looked like a taser.

\#

"Listen, I am just going to give you a chance Benny, stand down, go back to Las Vegas or much worse things will happen between my organization and you" continued Agent GA.

\#

"What do you mean by that, my father General Malik Dubious was brave enough to oppose the junta that ruled his country back in Mali, I think I am brave enough to fight the Blue Eagle Collective!" bellowed Benny.

\#

"Fine, have it your way" sighed Agent GA.

\#

The agent fired his taser gun, however, Benny was able to dodge the taser just in the nick of time. The agent couldn't believe he missed, Benny then rushed towards the agent and the two began to have a brawl on the ground.

Chapter One

<u>Shocked Hugo</u>

\#

Hugo Roth gazed at the brawl between Benny Dubious and Agent GA, neither was making a mark on each other as it reached a stalemate. Both were evenly matched, Hugo knew he had to tell the truth about "Moshie Scheinman" being a fake persona of his. He headed over towards the computer console and soon the music ceased which the entire crowd paused.

\#

"Uh, ladies and gentlemen, sorry to disrupt the concert but I have an announcement to make" said Hugo.

\#

Agent GA nodded in silence towards Hugo, Benny paused as well. The Malian crime boss knew he would have to make a mad dash towards where Samuel was to get him out instead of rescuing Hugo.

\#

"The Moshie Scheinman identity is a fake" continued Hugo.

\#

The crowd all gasped in horror.

\#

"You mean, you are NOT a real Jewish rapper?" remarked a woman within the crowd.

\#

Rabbis Isaac Green and Stephen Katz were no doubt disappointed in the back of the stage. They couldn't believe that they were swindled by someone pretending to be a Jewish rapper.

\#

"And here it's the anti-Semites that think we're the ones doing the swindling, but someone swindled us instead" laughed Rabbi Isaac.

\#

The two rabbis didn't know if the crowd was going to go on stage to chase after whoever this "Moshie" really was.

\#

<u>Accusing Samuel Roth!</u>

\#

Hugo then continued on with his speech about the "Moshie" persona being a lie, he then went to point fingers at his cousin - Samuel Roth.

\#

"This entire idea was pushed by Samuel Roth, my cousin who is running against Ms. Nia Hope Carver, the love of my life, though after this I am not sure if she'd care about me or join the mob" sighed Hugo.

\#

Hugo resigned in defeat awaiting further action from the crowd. Nia froze in horror realizing that the "Moshie Scheinman" was really Hugo Roth in disguise. Senator Amos Carver III chuckled to himself, he knew the truth the entire time.

#

"You have to get him out of there" whispered Ashura to Nia, "I do not know if the crowd will just form a horde to the stage."

#

Nia nodded and soon got up on the stage with Hugo, Hugo was nervous. It was the first time he was his real self in front of her, not some fake identity he made up.

#

"I should slap you right now, but I think we should leave" said Nia.

#

Nia felt a slap would be too much, even for Hugo.

#

"Just take me to your car and drive" said Nia.

#

Hugo was shocked Nia was okay with him being his usual self, for Benny he knew he had to reach Samuel as he pushed members of the crowd away.

#

<u>Samuel Tries to Escape</u>

#

The crowd at the concert were not angry at Hugo Roth for pretending to be Moshie Scheinman, instead some members of the crowd spotted Samuel Roth the main perpetrator behind it in the back.

#

"Hey, it's Samuel Roth, he's attending the concert!" said a man.

#

"Yea, he's the one who put up his cousin like that!" added a woman.

#

The crowd then began to boo Samuel and began to throw objects at him, his wife Josephine soon joined in with the crowd.

#

"Hey, let me join you guys, I didn't want my husband being involved in this" laughed Josephine.

#

Josephine took a few pieces of trash and began to toss it at her husband. It was only then that Benny Dubious arrived to shield Samuel along with the Jana brothers - Dev and Ojas trying to protect him.

#

"Uh, I guess I am not going to get that 100 million dollars from President Harold Truax" sighed Benny.

#

Samuel shook his head.

#

"Just get me out of here" said Samuel.

#

Benny provided most of the protection for Samuel, while Dev and Ojas provided additional cover. The four were able to escape the mob.

#

Hugo's Ride with Nia

#

Hugo said very little at first to Nia as they got into his car and started to drive off. Nia wanted to get back to her apartment after this ordeal was over.

#

"Just take me home" said Nia.

#

Hugo knew she hated him, it was unlikely she'd like him for who he truly was.

#

"I'm sorry this all happened, the name just came to me at that event" said Hugo.

#

"Why didn't you tell me you were Samuel's cousin to begin with, my father would have been okay with it" added Nia.

#

"I was nervous, I just made up the name" added Hugo.

#

"But you made things worse for you and your cousin" continued Nia.

#

Nia kept on nagging to Hugo as if they were still a couple, though Hugo was use to this brand of nagging by now as he saw it in Samuel and his wife Josephine. Nia didn't know if she should break up with Hugo because of this stunt.

#

"I'm not sure if I should breakup with you, you are quite handsome, but I would have to think about it" continued Nia.

#

"I, understand" said Hugo.

#

But as Hugo soon arrived at her apartment, Nia was surprised to find members of the Blue Eagle Collective spies gathering evidence.

Chapter Two

<u>Investigating Samuel Roth</u>

\#

Nia was shocked that she couldn't just leave to go back to her apartment. She could see the Blue Eagle Collective spies along with the regular police doing a search warrant trying to find the listening devices that Samuel had ordered Benny and Hugo to plant.

\#

"We found listening devices" said a Blue Eagle female spy to a police officer.

\#

The police officer gazed at Hugo's car as he was about to park. The officer signaled to lower down the window for Nia.

\#

"We're investigating Samuel Roth trying to tamper with your apartment, it's best you come back within a few hours say tomorrow morning" continued the police officer.

\#

"Tomorrow, but where would I—" sighed Nia.

\#

Nia groaned, she couldn't believe she would have to be staying at Hugo's place.

#

"You can always stay at my place" said Hugo.

#

Nia sighed as she had no other choice.

#

"Fine, take me to your place but no funny business" said Nia.

#

Hugo soon drove towards his apartment where the two soon got out. Nia was still furious with what transpired. However she would soon change her mind about Hugo as she soon got a surprised text message from her campaign manager.

#

<u>Nia Beating Samuel?</u>

#

Nia was surprised by the text message by Ashura Clark that she was ahead in the polls!

#

"That stunt that this Hugo Roth pulled off worked in your favor!" said Ashura, "I do not know how to explain it, but honesty does set someone free!"

#

Nia glanced over towards Hugo and showed him the text message.

#

"Your little stunt is costing your cousin the Senate race" said Nia.

#

"Well, I did met up with this spy from the Blue Eagle Collective who encouraged me to tell the truth" said Hugo.

#

Hugo didn't name Agent GA, but he knew that was the right timing that Agent GA mentioned. Nia soon hugged Hugo, even while he was still in his "Moshie Scheinman" attire.

#

"I can't believe it, but that act saved my campaign!" laughed Nia with joy, "I guess you are boyfriend material after all!"

#

"Really?" asked Hugo.

#

"Yes" replied Nia, "I have to call my father on this."

\#

Nia soon began to call up her father - Senator Amos Carver III who had arrived at his own apartment was pleased.

\#

"I am happy for you that you are doing well in the polls" said Senator Amos, "maybe you can succeed my legacy."

\#

"Yes, I certainly hope to become the next Senator" added Nia.

\#

Nia knew she would have to spend more time with the real Hugo Roth.

\#

The Real Hugo Roth

\#

The "Moshie Scheinman" persona that use to haunt Hugo Roth had all but disappeared. Hugo couldn't believe it but it felt like a weight over him had just been lifted.

\#

"I am so happy you are okay with me" said Hugo.

\#

"Yes" replied Nia, "it makes so much sense now that we should be together."

#

Nia was quite pleased that Hugo was his real self to her and not some impostor trying to pretend to be something else. The two began to cuddle on the sofa in Hugo's living room area of his apartment. As for Samuel, Samuel managed to drive out of there without his wife. He couldn't believe Josephine had joined the mob at the crowd.

#

"I am coming home on my own" said Josephine in a text message to Samuel.

#

Samuel swallowed, he knew that stunt would cost him the Senate race. He soon received another text message from an anonymous number - from President Harold Truax who wasn't happy.

#

"So disappointed that you are not ahead, I guess I was wrong to trust someone like you" said President Harold.

#

Samuel knew he would have to face the music with Josephine once she arrived home.

#

<u>Waiting for Josephine</u>

#

Benny Dubious along with the Jana brothers arrived at Samuel's house, they could see that their boss was quite nervous on what was going to transpire next.

\#

"This can't be good" said Dev.

\#

"Let's just provide some moral support for the boss" added Ojas.

\#

Benny and the Jana brothers soon headed towards the front door and Samuel welcomed them in.

\#

"Josephine will arrive likely later in the evening" continued Samuel.

\#

Samuel was tired, Benny and the Jana brothers could see the look in his face.

\#

"Boys, I also have bad news, that little stunt that Hugo pulled is going to cost me the entire election!" cried Samuel.

\#

"How are we going to fix it?" asked Benny.

\#

"Well, we can try to create some scandal between Hugo and Nia" said Dev.

#

"I think we tried that with the entire Moshie persona and it didn't work" added Ojas, "Hugo is far too honest."

#

Soon a car pulled up, Josephine was dropped off by one of the concert goers who agreed to give her a ride back to her place. Lucky she didn't bring the concert mob with her to Samuel's house.

Chapter Three

Upset Josephine

#

Josephine began to march up to her house, she was in a fit of rage with her husband's antics back at the concert. Poor Hugo she thought had to endure all of this! She immediately began unlock the door with a key she had to her house. There was a defining silence with Samuel, Benny and the Jana brothers as the door began to creek right open.

#

"SAMUEL!" bellowed Josephine as she closed the door, "SAMUEL WHERE ARE YOU, YOU COWARD!"

#

Samuel was right in the living room area of the house as she made her way through, she could see that her husband was frighten by her behavior.

#

"Please honey, I can explain all of this" said Samuel.

#

"You better, because I wouldn't be surprised if there would be police arriving at our house at any given moment to arrest you" continued Josephine.

#

Benny and the Jana brothers knew they better find their way out of Atlanta, Georgia fast.

#

"We better find our way out of town" whispered Dev to his brother Ojas and Benny.

#

"Yea, good idea" said Benny.

#

Benny tipped his hat to Samuel and soon began to head out but not before Josephine began to scold him and the Jana brothers.

#

<u>Not So Fast!</u>

#

Josephine was pretty enraged at Benny and the Jana brothers also being behind this little stunt of a fake concert. She couldn't believe how terrible her husband was putting Hugo in harm's way.

#

"YOU THREE ARE JUST AS GUILTY AS MY HUSBAND IS!" bellowed Josephine.

#

Benny smiled as he began to try to slide away, the Jana brothers did the same.

#

"GET BACK HERE!" bellowed Josephine.

#

But it was too late, the trio had managed to flee the house in the nick of time before Josephine continued to blow her gasket. It was rage that Samuel had never felt in years since he was married with her.

#

"AS FOR YOU" said Josephine as she turned towards Samuel, "I AM PREPARED TO GET A DIVORCE ATTORNEY TO FILE FOR A DIVORCE!"

#

Samuel was spooked by this sudden shift.

#

"A divorce?" asked Samuel.

#

"You heard me, a divorce!" bellowed Josephine.

#

The yelling could be heard all the way to the ears of Benny and the Jana brothers, Benny was going to share their car as they were going to head off.

#

"You better arrange your flight out of here while you can" added Ojas.

#

"I am on it" said Benny as he started to call up Zafar Mehmet.

#

<u>Alerting Zafar</u>

#

Zafar Mehmet was aware of the situation unfolding in Atlanta, Georgia even though he was as far off as Las Vegas. He could tell that Benny would soon require a flight home immediately.

#

"Benny, so glad that you are okay" said Zafar.

#

"Uh, even though I was in this for the money, it sounds like it's not worth it" added Benny.

#

"I understand" said Zafar, "I will arrange a private flight out of Atlanta that will happen as soon as tomorrow morning. I just need you to be at the airport."

#

"Yes, I will do just that, thank you Zafar" said Benny.

#

Benny was pleased his close associate Zafar could get him an immediate flight out of Atlanta, Georgia before anything happened to him. As Dev soon drove away from the Roth residence, he could see rows of unmarked cars moving in. No doubt they belonged to the Blue Eagle Collective. Agent GA had done his diligence in his investigation into Samuel Roth. He was leading the pack of Blue Eagle spies to the house.

#

"Here we are boys and girls let's get the party started" said Agent GA as he soon stepped out of the car.

#

Agent GA could tell he had just missed Benny and the Jana brothers by just a few minutes but Samuel was the main perpetrator they were after anyway.

#

<u>Blue Eagle Spies Search Samuel's Place!</u>

#

The Blue Eagle Collective was more professional than the FBI and the CIA put together, and more secretive in their investigations into their opponents. Agent GA soon burst through the door showing Josephine and Samuel a search warrant.

#

"SEE, YOU ALLOWED THIS TO HAPPEN TO YOURSELF!" bellowed Josephine.

#

Josephine was still nagging and yelling at her soon-to-be former husband. Samuel was squirming at her demeanor every step of the way. The Blue Eagle spies began to search the house top to button and found some listening devices inside Samuel's den.

#

"These are listening devices meant for wiretapping" said a male Blue Eagle spy to Agent GA.

#

"YOU WERE SPYING?!" cried Josephine in a fit of rage towards her husband.

#

Samuel said nothing as the regular police soon arrived at his house. Agent GA handed over the information towards the leading officer behind the case.

#

34

"Here you go, the civilian criminal court can take care of the rest" said Agent GA to the police officer.

#

"Thank you Agent GA" said the police officer.

#

Samuel sighed, he knew he was going to put away as he began to surrender himself to the police.

Part Two

36

Chapter Four

Shocking News!

\#

The news of Samuel Roth's arrest sent a shock wave throughout social media. Everyone was shocked but not surprised that Samuel had been arrested. Even supporters of former President Harold Truax who tried to support Samuel's futile campaign for the Senate. Nia along with her new boyfriend - Hugo Roth were in her apartment when at least a car of two Blue Eagle spies showed up.

\#

"We suspect there were listening devices planted in your apartment" said a female Blue Eagle spy.

\#

"Listening devices?!" cried Nia.

\#

Nia allowed the two spies to enter and surely enough they found the listening devices that Hugo and Benny had planted earlier. Hugo didn't know if he was going to get in trouble like his cousin Samuel.

\#

"Am I going to get in trouble for all of this?" asked Hugo.

\#

"No, you are safe, Agent GA needs your cooperation in this investigation" remarked a male Blue Eagle spy.

#

Hugo sighed with relief that he wasn't going to join his cousin Samuel in prison. It would have been too much for him to face jail after all the sort of ordeal that he went through.

#

Safe and Sound

#

After the two Blue Eagle spies left with the listening devices, Nia and Hugo sat down together on the sofa. They were happy being together, and found some quiet time since the concert.

#

"This has been moving so fast" said Hugo.

#

"I know, your cousin Samuel is in big trouble" added Nia.

#

"Yea, I can't believe Agent GA didn't want me to be behind bars" added Hugo.

#

"That's because you told him the truth back at the concert" added Nia.

\#

Hugo felt relieved that he wouldn't have to ever see his cousin Samuel again. For Samuel Roth, he soon found himself booked and placed in a temporary holding cell at the police station.

\#

"You are going away for quite sometime" said a police officer.

\#

Samuel said no word to the police as he was escorted into his cell. He knew he already lost Josephine and soon he was going to lose the public support at large. He could even imagine how disappointed former President Harold Truax must feel.

\#

"Uh, I can't believe I put Hugo through all of that" sighed Samuel as he sat it to himself while sitting in jail.

\#

Samuel would need sometime to think for what he did. As for Benny, it was time for him to try to leave Atlanta, Georgia the following morning.

\#

<u>Benny Preparing to Leave</u>

\#

Benny Dubious had managed to pack all of his luggage and checked out of the hotel. He called for a rider share service ride to the airport.

#

"Looks like you're in a hurry, I will make the trip quick" said the driver.

#

Benny got into the backseat of the car and the car drove off. He was thankful that nothing would happen to him but everything was sadly happening to Samuel. He took a glance on social media on his cellphone to see if there were any updates. Surely enough, Samuel was facing a judge and the judge wasn't pleased.

#

"I am very disappointed you resorted to spying on your opponent and putting your cousin through that terrible ordeal" said the judge, "your trial will begin after the election is over."

#

Samuel knew that he wouldn't be receiving any freedom anytime soon as he said nothing to the judge. He already was assigned an attorney, as no other attorney wanted to associate with his behavior. Josephine was also in the audience as well and was ready to serve him divorce papers.

#

"Here are the divorce papers, my attorney states I need your signature" said Josephine.

#

Benny couldn't believe how defeated Samuel looked in the footage.

\#

<u>Heading Home</u>

\#

Benny soon got onto his flight that was scheduled to head towards Las Vegas. He soon took his seat after putting his luggage away.

\#

"Have a safe flight to Las Vegas" said a flight attendant.

\#

Benny smiled at her, and sat back and relaxed. The flight soon took off, and away Benny was heading off from Atlanta, to Las Vegas. No more issues with the Blue Eagle Collective or so that he thought.

\#

"Yep, there is no chances for the Blue Eagle Collective to catch up to me" laughed Benny to himself.

\#

Benny sat back in a deep slumber and began to drift off, but as Benny continued to sleep he soon woke up in his own casino. He found a strange note written by someone he didn't recognize.

\#

"Hello Benny, I know what you did in Atlanta, my boss wants to go after you so desperately - Sincerely Agent NV" read the note.

#

The note in the dream was a mere warning to Benny on the consequences of his behavior. Agent NV did exist and she wasn't happy on what transpired in Atlanta, Georgia. Her main boss - Boss DC wasn't happy either.

#

Agent GA's Concerns

#

The investigation into Samuel Roth continued under the watchful eyes of Agent GA, while Benny was flying home to Las Vegas, Agent GA was discussing the matter with his counterpart - Agent NV a mysterious woman spy working for Boss DC. Boss DC oversaw all of the major spy operations of the Blue Eagle Collective and answered to the President Sebastian Baden. Agent GA was discussing the case in a disclosed office in downtown Atlanta. He had the image of a shadow figure of a woman and a man on Zoom.

#

"That Benny Dubious is a pest to our operations" said Boss DC.

#

"I understand sir, but he wasn't arrested with Samuel Roth" continued Agent GA, "only because he wasn't the brains of the operation."

#

"But he was promised money from the Red, White and Secure" continued Boss DC.

#

Boss DC was no doubt furious that Agent GA didn't go further than just arresting Samuel. He didn't even bother to get the Jana brothers arrested.

#

"Look, Samuel was the main perpetrator behind all of this, he's behind bars that's all that matters" continued Agent GA.

#

"I live close to Las Vegas, I know this Benny Dubious character and I can spy on his activities until I decide to strike" said Agent NV.

#

"Just be careful" said Boss DC, "this Benny Dubious is rather unorthodox in his approach. Try to lure him into some sort of fake operation to ambush him."

#

Boss DC had a few suggestions for Agent NV, for Agent GA his time with Benny was over.

Chapter Five

<u>No Consequences for Benny</u>

\#

The flight between Atlanta and Las Vegas which would be a long eight hour flight. Benny was thrilled nothing bad happened to him and was thankful he was getting out of Atlanta.

\#

"So happy to be on this flight" said Benny to himself.

\#

The passenger next to Benny didn't say a word at first, but noticed him from somewhere before.

\#

"Say, don't I know you from somewhere?" asked the passenger.

\#

"Uh, I just have that sort of face" chuckled Benny.

\#

Benny was doing his best trying to hide his image from the fake concert where he was ordered to rescue Hugo Roth. The passenger could have sworn Benny was from somewhere familiar.

\#

"I know you have to be from some familiar place" said the passenger, "but I just cannot put my mind onto it."

#

"Yea, I'm sure it will come up" said Benny, "just do not bother me for the rest of the flight."

#

The other passengers also had similar whispers among each other.

#

"Say, is that the crazy man from the fake concert?" whispered one woman.

#

"Yea, his white suit and hat gives himself away" whispered a man.

#

Benny ignored the comments from the passengers as the flight continued.

#

Back Home in Las Vegas

#

Meanwhile, back home in Las Vegas, Zafar Mehmet was doing a security check with his mansion. He didn't seem to trust the likes of the Blue Eagle Collective after Benny's mishap in Atlanta, Georgia.

Zafar had his own men regularly search the premise for any possible intruders.

#

"So boss, you are upset that the Blue Eagle Collective might send someone after you?" asked one of the men.

#

"I am worried that they will target Benny and me next, I am just taking the utmost precautions" continued Zafar.

#

The perimeters of the mansion were all regularly checked by the highly trained professionals that Zafar hired. Zafar had hired the Taran Guards from Turkmenistan, since Benny's attempt to appease a mysterious client also had affiliations with the same group. The Taran Guards were doing their best to try to make the mansion secure and safe.

#

"Nothing here sir" said a Taran Guard soldier as he checked the back entrance of the mansion.

#

"Everything is clear here" remarked another in the hallway.

#

Zafar was taking no chances, he could get the feeling whoever this mysterious Agent NV was she was on the prowl already in Las Vegas.

#

<u>Agent NV on the Prowl</u>

#

Agent NV was already on the prowl in Benny's home area in Las Vegas. Benny was vulnerable because he didn't have proper security assets yet. She was checking out his various casinos, it would be sometime before Benny's flight would arrive in Las Vegas' airport.

#

"This has to be the main casino" said Agent NV.

#

Agent NV was given orders by Boss DC to plant listening devices, she had managed to disguise herself as a cleaning lady for the casino which none of Benny's henchmen could find anything suspicious.

#

"Looks clear to me" said one of the henchman, "you are free to clean the casino."

#

Agent NV felt this was payback for what Benny did back in Atlanta, Georgia by helping Samuel Roth with his listening devices in Nia Carver's apartment. It would provide a way for Agent NV to examine all of Benny's moves because implementing the scheme to get back at him. As she arrived into Benny's main office, she could see Benny was fond of himself back in his days as the White Batch right-hand man to Khalid Jared Muhammad.

\#

"Disgusting" said Agent NV as she gazed over Benny's various pictures.

\#

She then began to plant the listening devices all over the office and soon left.

\#

Unsuspecting Benny

\#

Benny who was still heading back to Las Vegas was very much oblivious to what was transpiring in his own casino by Agent NV. He didn't seem to think the Blue Eagle Collective would be after him so fast. As the flight continued, Benny gazed out of the window.

\#

"Ah, yes, the clouds are so lovely" said Benny to himself.

\#

The passenger next to him was doing his best to keep it all to himself. He could have sworn Benny was at the concert from the posts from social media. The same crazy man that was knocking down patrons at the concert was sitting RIGHT NEXT to him!

\#

"I hope this flight ends" thought the passenger in his head.

#

The passenger was no doubt nervous being around Benny, he didn't know what Benny would do. But as the flight attendant soon passed them, she handed out the flight's meals to Benny and the passenger.

#

"Here you go, your meal for your flight" said the flight attendant.

#

"Thanks" said Benny.

#

It was a simple dinner meal of chicken for everyone on the plane, while the flight continued, Benny wondered how Hugo was doing now that his persona was exposed as a fraud.

#

<u>Hugo and Nia</u>

#

Back in Atlanta, things were oddly going well between Hugo and Nia. Their relationship had flourished thanks to Hugo being honest. She was rather grateful for his honesty. They were spending a few days in her apartment before venturing out into one of her events for her campaign. Even though she was going to win, since Samuel Roth was in jail, she was still being out there anyway.

#

"I am so happy that we're together" said Nia as the couple cuddled on the sofa.

#

"Yes, it's so nice being with someone I care about" added Hugo.

#

Nia was still receiving text messages from Ashura nagging her to continue her campaign.

#

"You shouldn't be spending too much with your new boyfriend" said Ashura in one text message, "I know he is honest about what he did but he nearly cost you your election."

#

Ashura on the other end was having trouble trying to reach out to Nia since she was so busy with Hugo. Ashura who was in her own apartment could still see that Samuel still had some support despite being in jail.

#

"Uh, I can't believe that man still has support even after what he did to Hugo" sighed Ashura.

#

There was much disbelief in Ashura over why someone like Samuel could have gotten away with it even while in jail.

Chapter Six

<u>Ashura Calling Senator Amos</u>

\#

Ashura decided to reach out to Nia's father - Senator Amos Carver III hoping to get through his daughter. The Senator knew his days were numbered as time was ticking each day that he would soon no longer be in his office.

\#

"Yes, this is Senator Amos, what can I do for you Ms. Ashura?" asked Senator Amos.

\#

"Your daughter is ignoring my text messages, she has a campaign!" bellowed Ashura.

\#

"Let her relax for a few days, she will reply to your text messages" said Senator Amos, "how many have you sent?"

\#

Ashura counted, there were so many she sent it was hard to count them all.

\#

"She has ignored them all" added Ashura.

#

"Well, maybe it's a good thing that Nia is being with Hugo, it shows the public that she is human like everyone else" added Senator Amos.

#

"And that's a good thing how?" asked Ashura.

#

"One thing for certain is, Nia wants to be just like everyone else" continued Senator Amos.

#

Ashura paused for a moment to get a grip on the Senator's words of wisdom for her.

#

"I guess I will wait, she will respond when she is ready" added Ashura.

#

"That's good to know" added Senator Amos.

#

The Senator was pleased that his daughter was taking up the mantle in continuing his legacy, he knew she'd beat Samuel Roth but didn't want things to be rushed like how Ashura wanted.

#

A Few Days with Nia

\#

Hugo spend a few days with Nia in her apartment, he ended up sleeping in the living room area since she had no extra bedrooms on the sofa. She could tell that he was much happier now that his cousin Samuel was in jail.

\#

"I see you are so much happier, you were too nervous pretending to please your cousin with that Moshie Scheinman persona" said Nia as she checked up on him.

\#

"Yea, I couldn't believe I made up that name right at that event" added Hugo, "uh, I feel so embarrassed by that."

\#

"I know how you feel" added Nia.

\#

Nia kissed Hugo on the cheek and then began to make breakfast for him. Hugo was appreciative he had a supportive girlfriend. Hugo didn't seem to care that much about his cousin Samuel being in jail. He only wished Samuel would have not pushed the envelope too much with the fake persona. Even the "Moshie Scheinman" persona that would often appear to Hugo was calmer because of it too.

\#

"So, your girlfriend accepts you for who you are?" asked Moshie.

\#

"Uh, yea, because I told the truth about you" added Hugo.

\#

"Makes sense" added Moshie.

\#

The ghost of the persona had become more of a watchful guardian to Hugo rather than an adversary.

\#

<u>Apologizing to the Rabbis</u>

\#

Hugo knew he had to make the call to the Rabbis Isaac Green and Stephen Katz, the two rabbis and their congregation were responsible for setting up most of the concert. They thought Moshie Scheinman was a legitimate figure. As Hugo made the call while Nia was making breakfast for him, Rabbi Isaac was just arriving at his synagogue when he heard the call straight from his own office in the synagogue.

\#

"Uh, wonder who could that be?" thought Rabbi Isaac.

\#

The rabbi soon picked up the phone, much to his surprise it was Hugo Roth on the other end.

#

"Hugo my boy, I am so glad you are safe and sound how are things with you?" asked Rabbi Isaac.

#

The rabbi wasn't mad at Hugo for telling the truth to the audience, he was more concerned about Hugo's safety especially with Benny Dubious pushing his way through the crowd.

#

"I am fine, I just wanted to take the time to apologize to you and Rabbi Stephen Katz over the whole entire Moshie Scheinman thing" said Hugo.

#

The apology wasn't easy for Hugo, but he felt he needed to get it off his chest to the rabbis.

#

<u>Hugo's Apology</u>

#

Before Hugo could make the proper apology, Rabbi Stephen Katz arrived at the synagogue and noticed Rabbi Isaac was on the phone. He signaled Rabbi Stephen to come in.

#

"It's Hugo on the other end, he wants to apologize to us" whispered Rabbi Isaac.

\#

"Yes, I guess I would accept whatever he says" added Rabbi Stephen, "so very concerning with the entire fiasco of the event. But I am glad they all turned against Samuel Roth for being the true culprit at fault."

\#

The rabbi soon placed the phone call on speaker.

\#

"Stephen has arrived, you may say your apology to both of us" added Rabbi Isaac.

\#

"Well, I just wanted to say I am sorry for what I have done in fooling the both of you into thinking that Moshie Scheinman was someone real" continued Hugo.

\#

"We both humbly accept your apology" said Rabbi Isaac, "you know you are very brave to oppose your cousin's political ambitions like that by outing him at the concert."

\#

"Yes, your bravery will not go unnoticed" added Rabbi Stephen, "we will make sure the rest of our congregation will hear this."

#

"Thank you sirs" said Hugo on the other end.

#

Hugo ended the call, he was rather pleased that the apology went better than expected.

Chapter Seven

<u>Making It Up to the Rabbis</u>

#

Hugo wanted to take things a step further between Rabbis Isaac and Stephen for how he tricked them into thinking he was "Moshie Scheinman" in disguise. Nia was listening into Hugo's plan.

#

"I would like to attend one of your sessions at your synagogue" continued Hugo on the phone with Rabbis Isaac and Stephen.

#

"You don't have to, the apology is more than enough" said Rabbi Stephen.

#

"That's a wonderful idea" added Rabbi Isaac, "even though Stephen clearly is okay with the apology, being at our synagogue is the next step for the healing process. I hope to see you this coming Friday."

#

"Will do" said Hugo.

#

Nia was impressed with Hugo's bravery on apologizing to the two rabbis for what he had done with the Moshie persona.

\#

"You are definitely not like your cousin Samuel" said Nia, "I would love to also be at the synagogue with you this Friday."

\#

"I just hope everyone at the congregation is so easy going like them" added Hugo, "you never know if there are those who have some resentment for what I have done."

\#

"I am sure if you explained yourself to them, they'd understand" added Nia.

\#

Nia was supportive of her boyfriend's actions to make amends with the two rabbis and their congregation. He was going to get this chance as the week progressed. Meanwhile, for Benny Dubious trouble was already starting when he arrived home in Las Vegas.

\#

Taran Guards Greet Benny

\#

Benny Dubious arrived safely back in his home of Las Vegas, the first thing Benny was ready to do was head towards his casino to check on the status. But as Benny exited the airport with his luggage, he noticed two strange soldiers holding up his last name "Dubious".

\#

"Uh, I am he, is there something wrong gentlemen?" asked Benny.

#

"You, Zafar wants you at his manor pronto it's an urgent matter" said the Taran soldier.

#

The two soldiers escorted Benny into the secured car they were driving and soon headed off. Benny was curious to know where the Taran Guards were from.

#

"Say, who sent you, I don't need protection" said Benny.

#

"We are from Turkmenistan, that mystery client of yours that asked to kidnap the talking komodo dragon not long ago had sent us" remarked the soldier at the wheel, "we have received intelligence that the Blue Eagle Collective is after you since your little stunt in Georgia."

#

Benny soon bursts out with laughter over the thought of being targeted by the Blue Eagle Collective.

#

"They're targeting me?!" chuckled Benny as he started to laugh.

#

The Taran Guards knew Benny would be highly uncooperative on terms of protecting him. It took the Taran soldiers to arrive at Zafar's manor about twenty minutes from the airport.

#

Zafar Concerned

#

Zafar soon emerged from the front door of the mansion, usually it was one of his butlers or other servants. But this was an urgent matter that Zafar needed to address Benny. He was waiting in the front entrance of his mansion with a row of other Taran Guard soldiers. Benny gasped as he could see the professional behavior of these soldiers before him. Once the car stopped, a Taran soldier soon led Benny out of the car with his luggage.

#

"Benny, I am so glad you came home safe and sound" continued Zafar as he gave Benny a hug.

#

"What's with all of the heighten security?" asked Benny.

#

"The Blue Eagle Collective, they have placed a contract on you!" continued Zafar.

#

Benny paused for a moment.

\#

"They don't have the capability of doing that at least on domestic soil" continued Benny.

\#

"From the sort of data I have gathered, they have a slew of secretive spies operating in the mist of the civilian population" continued Zafar, "they can pull something off against you in the coming days."

\#

Benny's tone soon changed, a sense of dread fell over him. He didn't know if he was being watched by the Blue Eagle Collective right now.

\#

Securing Benny

\#

Zafar soon escorted Benny inside his mansion, the Taran Guards looked around for anything suspicious as Zafar closed the door behind them.

\#

"You should stay here in my mansion for a few weeks until this blows over" continued Zafar.

\#

"Look, Zafar, I know I might have made myself a target of the Blue Eagle Collective back in Georgia, but there is no way they can legally get rid of him" continued Benny.

#

"They said the same thing about President Harold Truax, why do you think he has gone into hiding?" asked Zafar, "It's because the President is worried about his own safety."

#

"And you know this how?" asked Benny.

#

"Since I was received a pardon from him, and cost him his re-election bid, I have been kept up to date through an anonymous source within his inner circle" continued Zafar.

#

Benny was still confused by all of this.

#

"Look, I need sometime to rest from my trip" said Benny.

#

"The guest room is on the second floor of the mansion, you'd see more Taran Guards all over my mansion because of our situation with the Blue Eagle Collective" said Zafar.

#

Benny nods and soon heads upstairs to the guest room.

Part Three

69

Chapter Eight

<u>Benny Resting</u>

#

Benny Dubious soon arrived on the second floor in Zafar's mansion, a butler was kind enough to show Benny his guest room.

#

"This way sir" said the butler.

#

"There has been a lot of activity here since I was gone" said Benny.

#

"Sadly yes sir but not for the better" remarked the butler.

#

The butler and the other servants were also worried about the prospects of the Blue Eagle Collective spying on them. Zafar's hunch was right, just outside the mansion a woman in a mysterious cloaked suit was gazing at the mansion through some binoculars. Agent NV as she was known by the Blue Eagle Collective was assigned to watch over Benny for the time being until further orders were given to her.

#

"Uh, he has arrived at Zafar's mansion" said Agent NV.

#

Agent NV continued to gaze at the mansion from a safe distance, she could see a number of Taran Guard soldiers on patrol. It was going to make matters much more difficult for her to get past them. The government of Turkmenistan had some interest in helping Zafar and his associate Benny Dubious for some odd reason.

\#

Too Much Security

\#

Agent NV took down some notes and sent it to her main boss - Boss DC who was the head of the Blue Eagle Collective operations in Washington DC. Boss DC answered directly to President Sebestian Baden, a rival of President Harold Truax. The two Presidents have been in dispute since the last election on who won certain electoral states.

\#

"What do you have to report to me Agent NV?" asked Boss DC.

\#

Boss DC was communicating to her through his main DC office through an anonymous number he was sending text messages to his various agents.

\#

"Boss, the mansion is heavily guarded by the Taran Guards" continued Agent NV.

\#

"So, try to draw Benny out with one of our disposal assets" continued Boss DC, "there are plenty of choices be on the board. Pick one, anyone."

#

Agent NV thought for a moment, Vegas Trucking Company she thought would be a good answer.

#

"We have a smuggling operation going on with the Vegas Trucking Company" continued Agent NV, "I will lure Benny out of his hiding place by bringing up their money issue with Zafar."

#

Agent NV knew Zafar couldn't resist a trucking company not following orders to his shipping company's payments.

#

Giving Orders to Not Deliver

#

After visiting Zafar's mansion, Agent NV headed towards her own secretive lair which was just a few paces away from the dreaded Area 51. There she began to send out an anonymous order through the Vegas Trucking Company not to deliver to Zafar's shipping company. The operation was to disrupt Zafar's lifeline of money and force Zafar to use Benny as a tool to bring it back up.

#

"This should hopefully work" said Agent NV.

\#

A few moments later, truckers who were on the road that were loyal to the Vegas Trucking Company received the word. It was an odd order, but it sounded like it was coming from the top.

\#

"So the boss doesn't want us to deliver to this Zafar Mehmet fellow anymore" remarked one of the truckers to his buddies through an inner com.

\#

"Yea, it seems like that" added a second trucker.

\#

"Well, orders are orders" said a third trucker.

\#

It would take sometime for Agent NV's plan to divert the truckers to stop the shipments for Zafar. She would have to apply that to the other trucking companies that would eventually have a fake boycott against Zafar.

\#

The Fake Boycott Scheme

\#

A few days had passed with nothing exciting for Benny happening. Benny missed being in his own casino and his own home. He couldn't believe Zafar had dragged him away from all of that because of some concern from the Blue Eagle Collective.

#

"The nerve of Zafar being so worked up like that because of my activities back in Georgia" thought Benny in his own head as he looked up to the ceiling of his guest room.

#

Soon there was a knock at the door, as Benny got up he noticed it was Zafar. Zafar had a worried look on his face.

#

"Benny, someone is messing with my lifeline of money for my shipping company" said Zafar.

#

"But I thought you were secured enough" said Benny.

#

Zafar soon escorted Benny towards his office, there he showed Benny the data on the desktop computer.

#

"Someone is telling trucking companies to boycott my shipping company" continued Zafar, "I think the Vegas Trucking Company is the area to start on the main source. I know this sounds like a risk."

\#

"Hey, count me in for some action, I'm bored and I need something to do" laughed Benny.

\#

"Very well, you are to track down any of these truckers" continued Zafar, "of the Vegas Trucking Company. Demand answers to why they are boycotting my company."

\#

"Will do" said Benny.

\#

Zafar soon headed Benny towards the armory room within his mansion.

Chapter Nine

<u>Providing Benny with Protection</u>

#

Zafar soon gave Benny some armor to wear, especially a bulletproof vest. Benny was confused to why he would need something like this.

#

"Look, the Vegas Trucking Company is to believed to be one of the many fronts of the Blue Eagle Collective" continued Zafar, "you are going to need as much protection as possible."

#

"Alright, alright, I see you are serious about protecting me" said Benny.

#

Zafar then gave Benny a pistol with some ammunition.

#

"You will be needing this, you never know if those truckers are armed" added Zafar.

#

Zafar had every right to be concerned for Benny's safety as he was heading out. He then handed Benny the keys to one of his many cars.

#

"Benny, you may drive one of my cars to spy upon the Blue Eagle Collective's trucking scheme" said Zafar.

#

"Thank you" said Benny as he grabbed the keys.

#

Benny soon headed towards the garage area of the mansion and soon got into the car that the keys controlled. He soon began to drive right on off, Agent NV began to follow Benny on a motorcycle as he drove out of the gates of the mansion.

#

Feeling Followed

#

Benny was back in action, it was sometime since his adventure in Georgia that he was happy to be out. Being cooped up in a room all week wasn't his thing at all. But as he glanced in the mirror of Zafar's car he noticed a strange woman in a motorcycle.

#

"Must be a fan of mine" chuckled Benny.

#

Benny seemed to ignore that the woman was secretly Agent NV in disguise. She was wearing all black meant to be a cloaking suit. As Benny drove around the Las Vegas area he missed the smell of Vegas.

He was determine to search for the Vegas Trucking Company in the area.

#

"Now where are you, you pesky truckers" said Benny.

#

Benny continued to search for the truckers, but for some reason the only truckers that were on the road were meant for various supermarkets. Not the sort of thing for Zafar's business. But soon Benny found an unmarked truck that was parked outside a diner. It was strange for it to be out in the open like that.

#

"I wonder if that truck belongs to the Vegas Trucking Company" thought Benny to himself as he parked the car and got out.

#

Benny gazed at the truck and began to inspect it.

#

<u>Inspecting the Truck</u>

#

Benny continued to inspect the truck that was parked near the diner. He didn't think that much, but Agent NV who parked herself not far from the diner wanted to position herself. She could see that Benny made a huge mistake by coming out.

\#

"That man is such a fool" said Agent NV to herself, "how dare he humiliate Agent GA in that fashion back at the concert!"

\#

Agent NV had heard of how Benny tackled Agent GA back at the concert, and wanted to get even by even targeting Benny! She sat down in her position and got out her sniper rifle.

\#

"I will not let this man mock our Blue Eagle Collective" said Agent NV.

\#

Benny didn't realize there were consequences to his actions back in Georgia in helping Samuel and Hugo Roth. As Benny continued to inspect the truck, the trucker soon arrived back from having his meal.

\#

"Hey, who are you!" cried the trucker.

\#

The trucker soon produced a pistol before Benny.

\#

"I said who are you!" bellowed the trucker.

\#

Benny ducked around the truck, making it harder for Agent NV to get a good look at him.

#

<u>Benny and the Trucker</u>

#

The trucker was no doubt furious that someone was looking at his truck, Benny was hiding right behind it.

#

"Come on out you coward!" bellowed the trucker.

#

The trucker began to move towards the area where Benny was hiding. Benny knew he would have to take this risk as he could feel the trucker getting closer and closer, step by step. Soon the trucker made the mistake first, Benny tackled the trucker and the two began to fight. The fight made it difficult for Agent NV to aim her sniper rifle at Benny.

#

"Stand still you idiot!" cried Agent NV.

#

Agent NV was clearly having trouble trying to face off with Benny. But she tried to make the shot - BANG! However, she missed just by a few inches away from Benny. Benny gazed around trying to figure out where the shot came from. The trucker attempted to slug Benny, but Benny managed to hold him down.

\#

"Enough!" cried Benny.

\#

The trucker squirmed, and sadly surrendered to Benny.

\#

"I'm sorry, I'm just protective over my truck!" cried the trucker.

\#

"Why has your company boycotted Zafar Mehmet?" asked Benny.

\#

The trucker knew that name very well.

Chapter Ten

Trucker Confesses

\#

The trucker soon had no choice but to confess if he wanted Benny Dubious off his case for good. The sniper that had attempted to target Benny was long gone as Benny gazed around for the source of the shooting. Agent NV had managed to use her cloaking suit to get away.

\#

"We were told to boycott Zafar Mehmet's company" continued the trucker, "we were being given direct orders from our boss."

\#

Benny thought it was quite puzzling for a trucking company to boycott Zafar for no reason. There had to be some sort of catch to all of this.

\#

"I will go back and speak with Zafar over this" added Benny.

\#

But as Benny was going to head back to his car, police soon showed up because of the gunfight. Benny explained to the officers how he was attacked first by the trucker.

\#

"Thank you for that information citizen, we will handle it from here" said one of the police officers.

#

The police soon moved in to arrest the trucker, and Benny decided to head back to Zafar's mansion fast. He could tell that whoever was trying to target him, wanted him out of the picture.

#

Suspecting the Blue Eagle Collective

#

Benny soon arrived back at Zafar's mansion and soon parked the car. A Taran Guard soldier soon greeted Benny as he exited the garage, and more Taran Guard soldiers were stationed in the front of the mansion keeping watch.

#

"Did you have a nice trip?" asked a Taran soldier to Benny at the entrance.

#

"Uh, had a run in with a sniper but I made it out without a scratch" added Benny.

#

The Taran Guards soon allowed Benny into the mansion, and headed immediately towards Zafar's office. Zafar was still trying to get the Vegas Trucking Company and other trucking companies to continue doing business with his shipping company. Benny could see Zafar was quite busy on the phone.

#

"I demand you restart your connection with my business" said Zafar.

#

"I am sorry I cannot do that" said the representative on the other line.

#

The trucking companies were all being reluctant towards Zafar's business, he was losing millions of dollars each day. Benny soon arrived in his office.

#

"Uh, I will have to discuss this matter some other time" said Zafar.

#

Zafar soon ends the phone call and turns his attention towards Benny.

#

Who is Agent NV?

#

Benny sat down in Zafar's office as he pulled up a chair towards the Zafar's desk.

#

"What have you found while investigating the Vegas Trucking Company?" asked Zafar.

\#

"They were told to boycott your company" said Benny, "I suspect it's the Blue Eagle Collective telling them this."

\#

"They probably did this to lure you into a trap" continued Zafar, "you being targeted like that by a sniper. I suspect the agent who targeted you is the mysterious Agent NV, she is a woman sniper involved with the Blue Eagle Collective. That's all the information I know."

\#

"So how do we stop them from targeting me?" asked Benny.

\#

"You would have to dig deeper into their own background and threaten to expose their name to the public" continued Zafar, "the Blue Eagle Collective HATES it when the real name of a top ranking agent is leaked."

\#

"So I have to just find the name of this mysterious woman sniper, shouldn't be too hard" said Benny.

\#

"It's much harder than you think it is" added Zafar, "the spies know how to hide their identity and keep a very low profile."

#

"Nothing I can't handle" said Benny.

#

"I would be careful going to your own casinos" said Zafar.

#

Benny knew he had to check up on them, he wondered if this was the consequences of him being involved in that episode in Georgia. He wondered how Hugo Roth was doing since then. Back in Georgia, the day of the apology was arriving for Hugo to Rabbis Isaac and Stephen.

#

Apologizing to the Congregation

#

Hugo was nervous as he showed up in the synagogue with Nia Carver, Nia knew this would help cement her chances in winning the election against Samuel Roth.

#

"Just be yourself that's all you have to do" said Nia as she gave Hugo a hug.

#

Hugo felt Nia's warmth, and the couple headed towards their seats. The rest of the congregation at first didn't see Hugo as they began to sit down for the sermon for the two rabbis. Rabbi Isaac and Stephen soon emerged.

#

"We are gathered here today because a young man wants to say something to us" said Rabbi Isaac, "Mr. Hugo Roth, would you please come up to the podium?"

#

Hugo held his breath as he stood up and headed over, he gazed over the congregation. He could see none of them had angry faces on them at all.

#

"I would like to take my time to thank you all for coming to this session, because I would like to apologize to you all for that fake concert you helped organized thinking that Moshie Scheinman was a genuine Jewish rapper when he wasn't" continued Hugo, "I made up that name at my girlfriend's event because I was nervous. Didn't think my cousin Samuel would try to use me."

#

The congregation were in awe with Hugo's bravery, they had a sense of closure this young man was willing to be honest with them.

Chapter Twelve

<u>Honest Hugo</u>

#

The rest of the crowd stood up and began to cheer Hugo's bravery.

#

"I must say that was pretty brave of you coming out here like this" said an old man among the congregation.

#

"Yes, no one has been that honest and moving as you" added an old woman.

#

"I wish there were more people like you in the world" said one man in the audience.

#

Hugo felt relieved that the congregation were happy. He could tell that there was closure for Nia as she had a happy smile on her face. After a few more moments of cheering by the congregation, Hugo soon sat down back in his seat. He then began to cuddle with Nia as the two rabbis continued their sermon.

#

"I am proud that you were brave enough to make that stand" said Nia as she whispered to Hugo.

#

"Yes" said Hugo, "I was nervous at first, but I think everyone gets the picture that I am sorry for what I did."

#

The sermon continued for the next few hours, after everything was over it was time to take Nia back to her apartment.

#

Dropping Nia Off

#

Hugo had to run a few errands for the rest of the day, as he dropped off Nia at her apartment she was rather pleased with him for the rest of the day.

#

"I hope to see you tomorrow" said Nia as she gave Hugo a kiss on the cheek.

#

"Yes, yes I will" said Hugo.

#

Hugo soon drove off, as he continued to drive off he noticed the coffee shop where he met Agent GA and noticed the agent sitting at his usual spot. Hugo got decided to pay the agent a visit and parked his car. Agent GA was surprised to see Hugo at the coffee shop on his own accord.

#

"I see things are back to normal with you, no more Moshie Scheinman persona issues?" asked Agent GA as he sipped his cup of coffee.

#

"Nope, haven't seen my persona that much" added Hugo as he decided to sit down.

#

"You know, the Blue Eagle Collective could use someone as sly as you" continued Agent GA, "how would you like to sign up to be one of us?"

#

"Really, me?" asked Hugo.

#

"Why not, you nearly fooled everyone with that persona of yours" added Agent GA.

#

"I accept the offer" said Hugo.

#

"Excellent, I will get the paperwork and send it to your apartment" said Agent GA.

#

Agent GA was pleased to find another recruit for the Blue Eagle Collective, he had high hopes for Hugo Roth. As for Benny Dubious, trouble was just getting started for his next chapter.

#

Paranoid Benny

#

Meanwhile, in Las Vegas, much to the advice of Zafar Mehmet, Benny decided to check up on his main casino. He parked his car outside the casino and headed inside. Nothing was amiss, the rest of the workers were busy with the customers of the casino.

#

"How was your trip to Georgia?" asked a casino worker.

#

"Uh, fine" said Benny.

#

Benny knew he wasn't going to get paid for that attempted service for the Red, White and Secure. He knew a more urgent matter had to be taken care of. As he headed up towards his office, he was unaware that listening devices had been planted by Agent NV. She was already listening in his every move from a disclosed area in downtown Las Vegas.

#

"Home sweet home" said Benny as he gazed around his main office.

#

Nothing was out of place, he sat down and began to try to relax for the rest of the day in his casino. Unsure of how Agent NV knew his every step. Would Benny find out the mysterious identity of Agent NV? Would Benny reveal her name? That would have to be in the next series. Until next time...

* * *

Don't miss out!

Visit the website below and you can sign up to receive emails whenever Maxwell Hoffman publishes a new book. There's no charge and no obligation.

https://books2read.com/r/B-A-JVYOC-IZDDF

BOOKS 2 READ

Connecting independent readers to independent writers.

About the Author

I graduated from California State University with a BA in History. I am fond of historical fiction, science fiction, fantasy, and horror.
Read more at https://www.instagram.com/vader7800/.

About the Publisher

I graduated from California State University of Northridge with a BA in History. I am fond of fantasy, science fiction, historical fiction and horror.

Read more at https://www.instagram.com/vader7800/.